THIS BOOK
BELONGS TO:

....

First Edition
ISBN-13: 978-1-62395-439-0
Hardcover: 978-1-5324-1060-4
eISBN: 978-1-62395-443-7
Published in the United States by Xist Publishing
www.xistpublishing.com
PO Box 61593 Irvine, CA 92602

WHO'S COMING FOR DINNER, LITTLE HOO?

FOR BUG.
LOVE, MOM.

BRENDA PONNAY

KNOCK! KNOCK!

WHO'S AT THE DOOR,

LITTLE HOO?

It's Grandma Hoo!

She brought cranberry stuffing!

KNOCK! KNOCK!

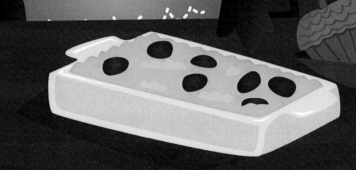

WHO'S AT THE DOOR,

Little Hoo?

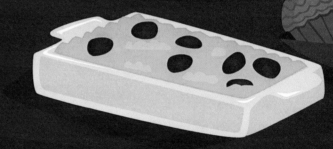

It's Gray Squirrel!

He brought
nut soup!

KNOCK! KNOCK!

WHO'S AT THE DOOR,

Little Hoo?

It's Wooly Bear!

He brought mashed potatoes!

KNOCK! KNOCK!

WHO'S AT THE DOOR,

LITTLE HOO?

It's White Cat!

She brought catnip salad!

LITTLE HOO?

It's Papa Hoo!

and his friend,

STRUT THE TURKEY!

LET'S EAT!

About the Author

Brenda Ponnay is the author and illustrator of several children's books including the Time for Bunny series and Secret Agent Josephine series. She lives in Southern California with her daughter, Bug* who inspires her daily.

You can read all about their crazy adventures on her personal blog: www.secret-agent-josephine.com

*Not her real name.

Make your own dancing turkey!
Visit www.xistpublishing.com/LittleHoo
to download this image then cut along the lines
and place your fingers through the holes to make
your turkey dance.